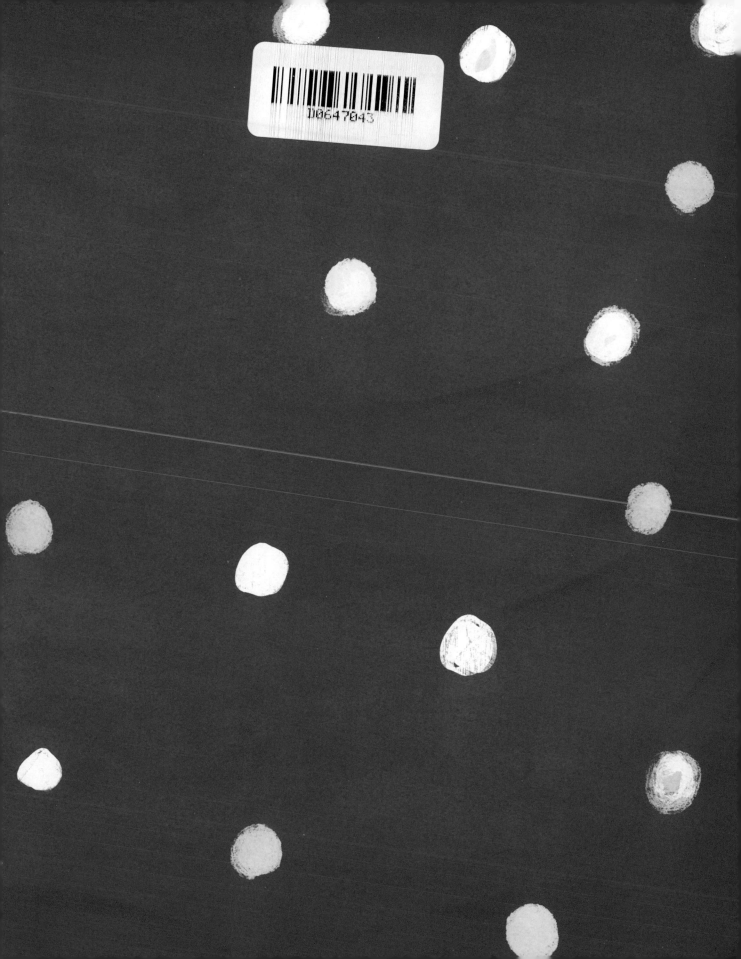

BEST BUDDIES

BY LYNN PLOURDE

ILLUSTRATED BY ARTHUR LIN

CAPSTONE EDITIONS
a capstone imprint

Best Buddies is published by Capstone Editions, an imprint of Capstone.
1710 Roe Crest Drive
North Mankato, Minnesota 56003
www.capstonepub.com

Library of Congress Cataloging-in-Publication Data
Names: Plourde, Lynn, author. | Lin, Arthur, illustrator.
Title: Best buddies / by Lynn Plourde ; illustrated by Arthur Lin.
Description: North Mankato, Minnesota : Capstone Editions, an imprint of Capstone, [2021] | Audience: Ages 3-5. | Audience: Grades K-1. |
Summary: A boy with Down syndrome and his dog are best friends, but how will they manage being apart when the boy heads to school for the first time?
Identifiers: LCCN 2021002307 (print) | LCCN 2021002308 (ebook) | ISBN 9781684461431 (hardcover) | ISBN 9781684461448 (pdf) | ISBN 9781684463992 (kindle edition)
Subjects: CYAC: Dogs--Fiction. | Friendship--Fiction. | First day of school--Fiction. | Down syndrome--Fiction. | People with mental disabilities--Fiction.
Classification: LCC PZ7.P724 Bg 2021 (print) | LCC PZ7.P724 (ebook) | DDC [E]--dc23
LC record available at https://lccn.loc.gov/2021002307
LC ebook record available at https://lccn.loc.gov/2021002308

Designed by Nathan Gassman

Printed in the United States   4654

FOR ISRAEL, ONE OF
OUR FAMILY'S BEST BUDDIES
—LP

TO ABBEY & BLUE, WITH LOVE
—AL

They met the day the boy
came home from the hospital.

So many smells.

So many sounds.

So many naps.

While the boy's mom and dad were busy with showers and shaving, *someone* had to babysit.

At snack time, they shared.
That's what best buddies do.

Once in a while, one of them needed a boost.

And they both thought car rides were relaxing.

The best buddies looked out for each other.
When one was lost, the other one found.

When one was forgotten,
the other one remembered.

The best buddies went on vacation together.

Enjoyed celebrations.

And snuggled at bedtime.

Like cake and frosting, the best buddies
always stuck together . . .

. . . until the boy started school.
A bus came and swallowed him up.

That first day, they both tried to be strong.

But there were tears.

And whining.

And moping.

And waiting . . .

. . . for that bus to spit the boy back out.

And when it did,
a tumble of joy!

They wouldn't let the other out of sight.

Not for a single second.

That night, they tossed and turned
and turned and tossed.

And couldn't fall asleep.

The next morning, one had a bellyache.
The other couldn't eat.

Feeling sad got all mixed up with feeling sick.
Mom and Dad said, "Give it a try."

Before the bus came,
the boy gave his best buddy
a bigger-than-big hug.

Such a big hug that
something fell off.

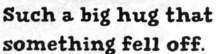

The boy held on to
it tight and smiled.

He ran back into the house
and returned with something
special for his buddy.

And then, they gave it a try.

It still was a long day apart.
But when they missed each other,
they smelled the best smell and felt better.

They were able to play.

And eat.

And even make a few new friends.

When the bus door opened,
they held on tight to each other.

And that's all that matters when you're . . .

. . . BEST BUDDIES.

About the Author

Lynn Plourde is the author of 40 children's books, including *The Boy Whose Face Froze Like That*. Some of Lynn's other titles include *Pigs in the Mud in the Middle of the Rud, Wild Child,* and her middle grade novel *Maxi's Secrets (Or What You Can Learn from a Dog)*, inspired by her best buddy, Maggie. Lynn does many author visits to schools each year, during which she teaches students how to write their own stories. Before becoming a full-time author, she worked for 21 years as a speech-language therapist in public schools, including working with many students with Down syndrome. Lynn lives with her husband in Winthrop, Maine, where she enjoys going for walks, gardening, reading, and playing with her young grandson. Visit her at www.lynnplourde.com.

About the Illustrator

Arthur Lin is an artist based in San Francisco, drawn by the storytelling of Sunday comics and various children's books. He received his master's degree in illustration in 2010 and has been illustrating books ever since. As a brand-new father, he was fortunate to capture the funny interactions between his newborn and dog, which provided a lot of inspiration for this story. Although they don't always get along, they are already best buddies!

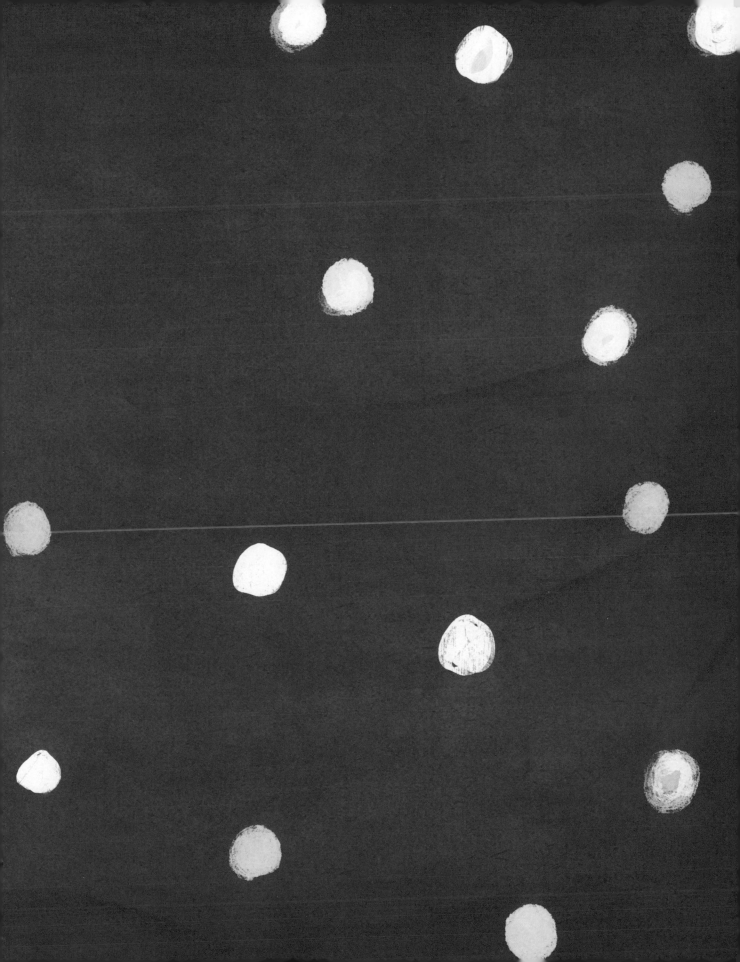